This and That

The Sound of TH

By Peg Ballard

The Child's World®, Inc.

This dog is big.

That dog is small.

This book is thick.

That book is thin.

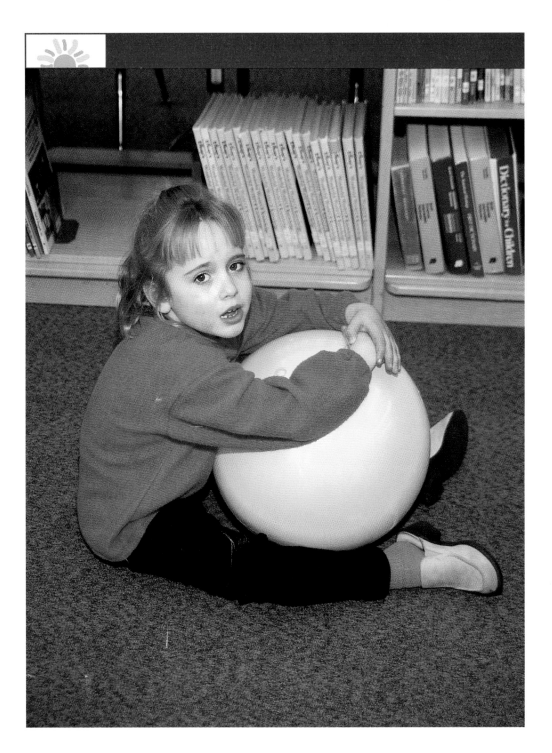

10

This ball is big.

That ball is small.

This pad is thick.

That pad is thin.

This box is big.

That box is small.

Word List

that

thick

thin

this

Note to Parents and Educators

The books in the Phonics series of the Wonder Books are based on current research which supports the idea that our brains are pattern detectors rather than rules appliers. This means children learn to read easier when they are taught the familiar spelling patterns found in English. As children encounter more complex words, they have greater success in figuring out these words by using the spelling patterns.

Throughout the 35 books, the texts provide the reader with the opportunity to practice and apply knowledge of the sounds in natural language. The 10 books on the long and short vowels introduce the sounds using familiar onsets and rimes, or spelling patterns, for reinforcement. For example, the word "cat" might be used to present the short "a" sound, with the letter "c" being the onset and "-at" being the rime. This approach provides practice and reinforcement of the short "a" sound, as there are many familiar words made with the "-at" rime.

The 21 consonants and the 4 blends ("ch," "sh," "th," and "wh") use many of these same rimes. The letter(s) before the vowel in a word are considered the onset. Changing the onset allows the consonant books in the series to maintain the practice and reinforcement of the rimes. The repeated use of a word or phrase reinforces the target sound.

The number on the spine of each book facilitates arranging the books in the order that children acquire each sound. The books can also be arranged into groups of long vowels, short vowels, consonants, and blends. All the books in each grouping have their numbers printed in the same color on the spine. The books can be grouped and regrouped easily and quickly, depending on the teacher's needs.

The stories and accompanying photographs in this series are based on time-honored concepts in children's literature: Well-written, engaging texts and colorful, high-quality photographs combine to produce books that children want to read again and again.

Dr. Peg Ballard
Minnesota State University, Mankato

23

Photo Credits

All photos © copyright: Romie Flanagan/Flanagan Publishing Services, except Photri: 2; Tony Stone Images: 5 (Dale Spartas).

Photo Research: Alice Flanagan
Design and production: Herman Adler Design Group

Library of Congress Cataloging-in-Publication Data

Ballard, Peg.
    This and that : the sound of "th" / by Peg Ballard.
    p. cm. — (Wonder books)
    Summary: Simple text about opposites and repetition of the letters "th" help readers learn how to use this sound.
    ISBN 1-56766-728-7 (alk. paper)
    [1. English language—Synonyms and antonyms Fiction. 2. Alpabet.]
  I. Title. II. Series: Wonder books (Chanhassen, Minn.)
    PZ7.B21195Th   1999
    [E]—dc21   99-15888
                                       CIP